D0537010

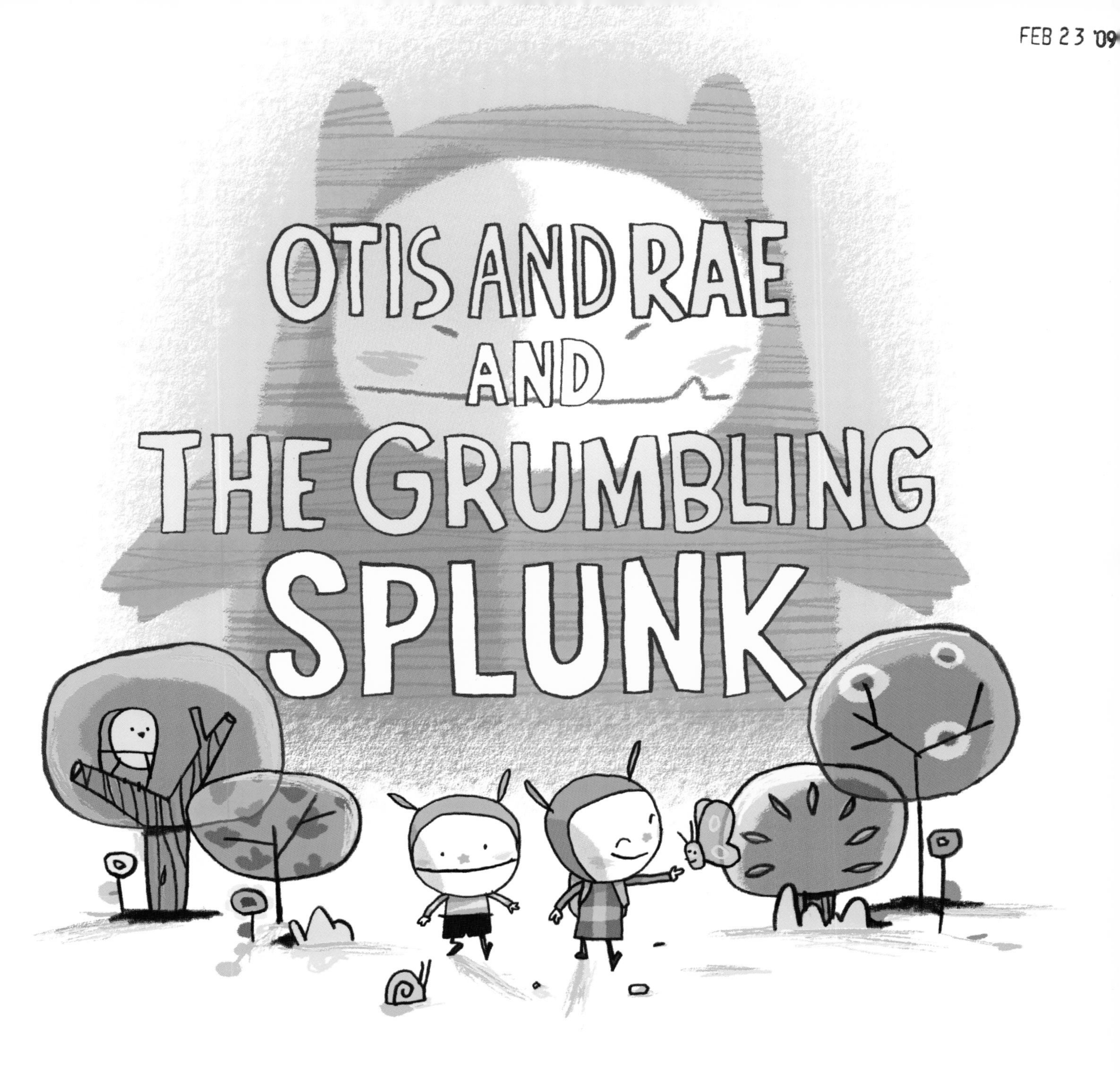

Laura & Leo Espinosa

Houghton Mifflin Company
Boston 2008

To Ben, Sofia, and Hannah

— L.E. and L.E.

www.houghtonmifflinbooks.com

The text of this book is hand lettered.
The illustrations are mixed media (pencil, coffee, gouache, and Photoshop).

Library of Congress Cataloging-in-Publication Data

Espinosa, Laura.
Otis and Rae and the Grumbling Splunk / written by Laura Espinosa and illustrated by Leo Espinosa.
p. cm.
Summary: While on their first camping trip ever, Rae looks forward to tracking a wild beast but it is a fearful Otis who first encounters the Grumbling Splunk, whose grumbling might not be so scary after all.
ISBN-13: 978-0-618-98206-6 (hardcover)
ISBN-10: 0-618-98206-X (hardcover)
[1. Camping—Fiction. 2. Monsters—Fiction. 3. Fear—Fiction.] I. Espinosa, Leo, ill. II. Title.
PZ7.E74667Oti 2008
[E]—dc22
2007012925

Printed in Singapore
TWP 10 9 8 7 6 5 4 3 2 1

One perfectly perfect summer day, Otis and Rae set out on their very first camping trip ever.

"Yessirree, Otis—this is it!" said Rae, taking it all in.

"Yeah, maybe," said Otis. "But I can't wait to set up camp and unpack those PB&B sandwiches."

Otis was always hungry for PB&B.

There's more to life than food, Otis. We could track a real live wild beast.
THE BIGGER, the better!
SSTOP!
begged Otis.
(He wasn't particularly wild about wild animals.)
I mean, this looks like a pretty good spot to put up the tent.
Why, yes. It's marvelous.

So, Otis and Rae unpacked,
set up their tent,
and made a campfire.
Otis feasted on his
favorite sandwiches
while listening to Rae weave
fantastical and scary stories
about the animals
that lived in the woods.

"OTIS, DID I EVER TELL YOU ABOUT THE MYSTERY OF THE GRUMBLING SPLUNK? WELL, WHEN THE MOON IS FULL AND YOU CAN SEE YOUR REFLECTION IN THE — "
Oh, my. Look at the time!
It's . . . getting pretty late and maybe we should go to bed.
7:30
Yes, Otis, you're absolutely right!
The early bird catches the worm and all that.
Hey, wait for me!

Rae fell fast asleep.
Otis tried and tried,
but he could not.

The chirping crickets and the beastly stories kept Otis wide awake.

CHIRP

CHIRP

CHIRP

CHIRP

CHIRP

Chirp

Then, suddenly, the chirping stopped.

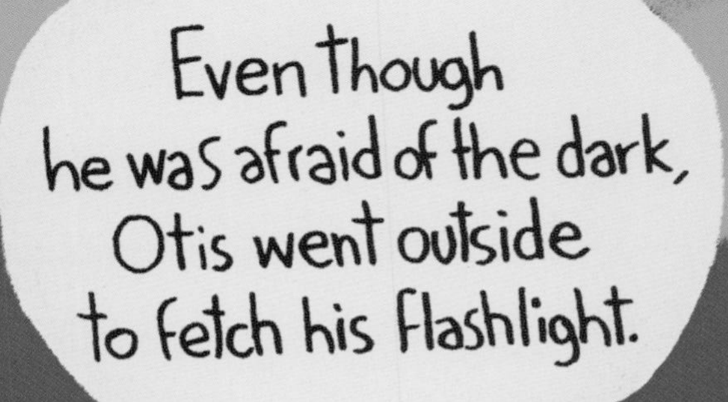
Even though
he was afraid of the dark,
Otis went outside
to fetch his flashlight.

WHAT
A
MESS!
I know
it's around here
somewhere.

Oops!
WHAT'S
THIS?

Bingo!

GRRR

RRRUMMBLE!

It was the scariest thing Otis had ever seen, and he ran as fast as he could away from it. And the scariest thing Otis had ever seen ran as fast as it could away from Otis.

Otis told Rae
all about the scariest thing
he'd ever seen.
"I think it might have been
that grumpy skunk
you told me about.
We better get out of here...
fast!"

"GRUMBLING SPLUNK,"
corrected Rae
as she jumped out of
her sleeping bag.
Which way did he go?
Rae, wait! Come back!
Are you CRAZY?

That way.
I mean, that way.
But you're **not** thinking...
You're going to get us bothAAHH

At that very moment
Otis and Rae fell down
into a dark ravine—
a very dark,
very deep ravine—
rolling and tumbling
as they went.
OUCH!

OUCH!!
OUCH!
OUCH!
OUCH!!
Oh, dear.
Where are we?

LOOK, OTIS!
We found ourselves a real live Splunk!

BONK!

Ouchy! That must have **hurt**.
IT'S OKAY, BIG GUY!
"I have just the thing," said Rae.
And she did.

The Splunk
was feeling better
in no time.
Now
all we need to do
is find our way
out of here.

But that wasn't so easy.
They walked and walked,
but the more they walked,

the more they felt like they were going in circles.
And they were.

Then Otis had an idea.
Hold up just a second, everyone!
OTIS EXPLAINED HIS PLAN AND THEY ALL AGREED IT WAS WORTH A TRY.

First, Rae climbed up to the tippy top.
Hold on tight!
Next, Otis, with a running hop, jumped and landed—
KURPLOP!
It was a good idea! Now Otis could see for miles.
Hey, there's our tent!

Carefully, they made their way back to the campsite.
A little to the left.
That's it.
Now go right.
Straight on.
WOOHOO! WE MADE IT!

WHAT A RIDE!
Boy, am I hungry!
See you around, Splunky.
It really was an honor to meet you.
I have one last question:
Why is it they call you the **Grumbling** Splunk?
GRRUMBLE

Zörry!
You know, Otis, I think our new friend might just be a little HUNGRY.
Why don't you join us for an early-morning snack?

So, Otis and Rae
and the Grumbling Splunk
sat down around the campfire
and ate PB&B sandwiches.

THE END

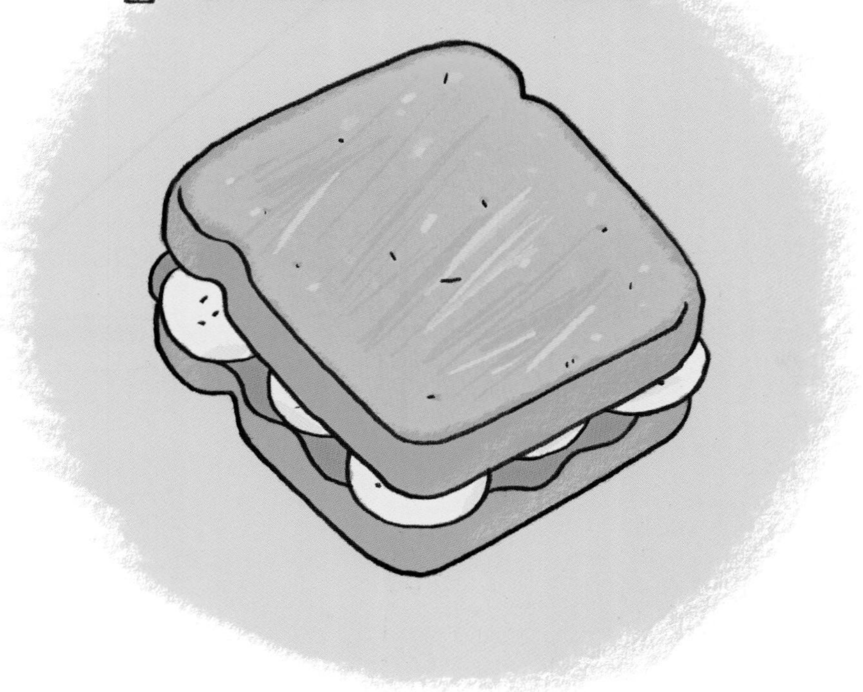

Answer: Peanut Butter and Banana